THE HOPI

ELAINE LANDAU

THE HOPI

Franklin Watts New York Chicago London Toronto Sydney A First Book

Map by Joe LeMonnier
Cover photograph copyright © Ben Klaffke

Photographs copyright ©: Ben Klaffke: pp. 3, 36, 38, 39; National Park Service, Wupatki-Sunset Crater National Monuments: p. 10; University of California Library, California Historical Society, Title Insurance and Trust Photo Collection: pp. 17, 19, 20, 30, 37; Leo deWys Inc. NY/Henryk T. Kaiser: pp. 12, 48; John Running: pp. 24, 55; Smithsonian Institution: p. 25 (41830-A); The Milwaukee Public Museum: p. 26; Artwerks/Jerry Sinkovec: pp. 29, 32; North Wind Picture Archives, Alfred, Me.: pp. 42, 53; Stock Montage/Historical Pictures Service: p. 44; Sam Roberts: p. 47; Southwest Museum, Los Angeles: p. 51 (N.35608); Colorado Historical Society: p. 54; Jim Markham: p. 58.

Library of Congress Cataloging-in-Publication Data

Landau, Elaine.
The Hopi / by Elaine Landau.
p. cm. — (A First book)
Includes bibliographical references (p.) and index.
ISBN 0-531-20098-1 (hrdcover). — ISBN 0-531-15684-2 (trd pbk)
1. Hopi Indians — History — Juvenile literature. 2. Hopi Indians — Social life and customs — Juvenile literature. [1. Hopi Indians. 2. Indians of North America.] I. Title. II. Series.
E99.H7L28 1994
979.1'004974 — dc20 93-31964 CIP AC

Printed in the United States of America
6 5 4 3 2 1

CONTENTS

THE HOPI

INTRODUCTION

In the 1830s mountain men hired to open a passageway between Santa Fe, New Mexico, and California told a fascinating story as they sat around their campfires. While scouring the surrounding territory, a few of the men claimed to have come across a village built high into the region's rocky cliffs. People obviously lived there, but no one was in sight.

The workers assumed that this was a small group of British people who had left their homeland many years ago and inhabited the area. These people were so peace loving that they didn't want the outside world to disrupt their lives. When anyone approached, they quickly hid themselves in nearby caves, where they remained until the intruders left.

THE RUINS OF AN ANCIENT HOPI SETTLEMENT. HOPI VILLAGES SEEM TO BE PART OF THE MESA BECAUSE THEIR COLOR AND OUTLINE REFLECT THE NATURAL ENVIRONMENT.

Of course, the workers' tale isn't true. British families never stayed in this town that almost seemed carved out of rock. Yet without knowing it they correctly guessed that they had come across a band of peaceful people. The workers had accidentally stumbled onto a Hopi Indian village.

The Hopi are a tribe of Pueblo Indians living in northeastern Arizona. In the 1500s Spanish explorers who found these native people noticed that they lived in villages that looked like Spanish towns. Because the word *pueblo* means "town" in Spanish, they called them Pueblo Indians. Although the different groups of Pueblo Indians are unique, they share some common traits.

Most Pueblos live in New Mexico along the Rio Grande and in the central west and western portion of the state. The Hopi, however, who live the farthest west of these Indians, inhabit three fingerlike cliff extensions of a high plateau known as Black Mesa. There individual Hopi villages perched on what's known as the First, Second, and Third Mesa look down on the desert plain below.

For centuries the Hopi have had a special bond to the earth. As their leaders put it, "It is here on this land that we are bringing up our younger generation and through preserving the ceremonies are teaching

LIFE ON BLACK MESA (SHOWN HERE), A HIGH PLATEAU IN NORTHERN ARIZONA. THEIR HOMES ARE AT AN ELEVATION OF ABOUT 6,000 FEET.

them proper human behavior and the strength of character to make them true citizens among all people."

The word Hopi means "peaceful." Yet, when necessary, they have fought for their people in various ways. Theirs is a tradition of strength and wisdom. This is the story of how they lived and fared before and after the whites came.

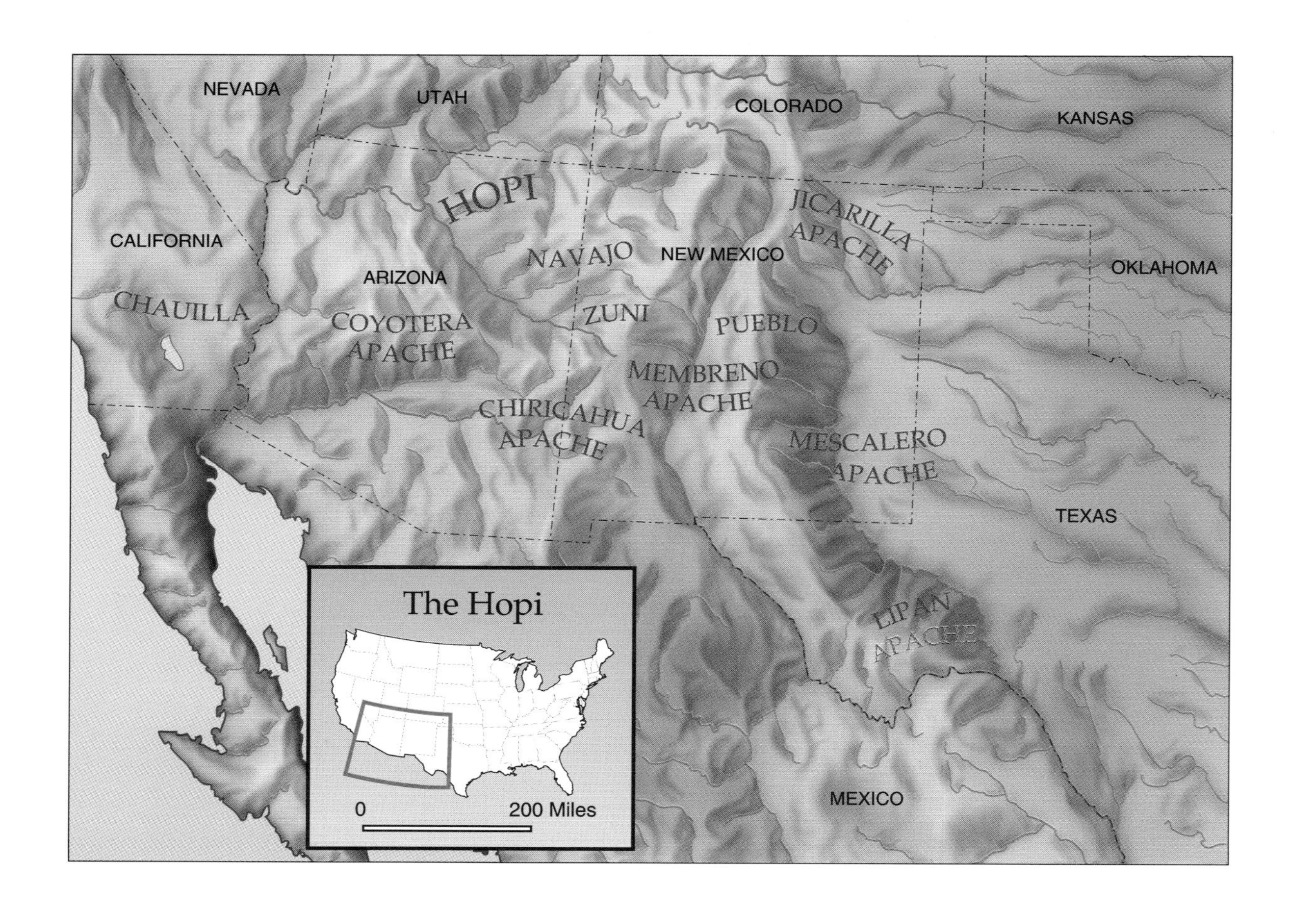

NEVADA
UTAH
COLORADO
KANSAS
HOPI
CALIFORNIA
NAVAJO
NEW MEXICO
JICARILLA APACHE
ARIZONA
OKLAHOMA
CHAUILLA
COYOTERA APACHE
ZUNI
PUEBLO
MEMBRENO APACHE
CHIRICAHUA APACHE
MESCALERO APACHE
TEXAS
LIPAN APACHE
MEXICO
The Hopi
0
200 Miles

HOPI FAMILIES AND HOMES

Traditional Hopi society was based on broad family groups, or *clans*. Each clan was made up of a number of families and bore the name of a bird or animal. Among these were the Bear Clan, Parrot Clan, Eagle Clan, Badger Clan, Spider Clan, Coyote Clan, Snake Clan, and others. A clan also had a special spirit protector, or *kachina*, and was represented by a stone or wood symbol known as a *tiponi*.

Because clan membership was passed on through women, newlyweds lived either with or near the bride's family. Husbands worked with their in-laws farming the family's fields and doing necessary repairs on their dwellings. Hopi never married within their own clan, and children were considered members of their mother's clan.

Even though a son remained with his wife's family after marrying, he thought of his mother's and sister's household as his true home. He frequently returned there to take part in ceremonies and instruct younger family members.

A traditional Hopi household usually included several clan-related families. They often lived together in a single house or a house to which several extensions were added. As the family grew still larger, its members moved to separate nearby houses. Those occupying the dwelling recognized as the clan house, however, were responsible for the clan's possessions. They also made sure that the clan fulfilled its ceremonial duties. This was essential because Hopi life centered on clan cooperation for the general welfare of the entire population.

A Hopi clan house was usually managed by an older clan woman and her brother. Age was not as important as the person's abilities, interest, and involvement in clan activities. All Hopi children were instructed in their clan's history, duties, and ceremonies. Those who seemed best suited to carrying on these traditions received more specific instructions.

The richness of Hopi life depended on the clan. It provided a broad base for sharing responsibilities and completing necessary tasks. Hopi children viewed their mother's sisters as their own mothers. Young

HOPI WOMEN SHOWN HERE ARE WORKING ON THE ADOBE HOMES THEIR FAMILIES LIVE IN. NOTICE THE BUILDING'S VARIOUS LEVELS.

people were as close to their cousins as to their brothers and sisters. Family clan members helped both in raising the children and in caring for the sick and aged. Housekeeping, farming, and other work was divided up in much the same way.

Clans also united the Hopi because the large and prominent clans existed in each village. They provided the native people with a continuing stream of relatives and an important sense of belonging. A Hopi who journeyed to another Hopi village found himself welcome in the households of his clan members.

The Hopi lived in houses of stone and adobe mortar. These clustered homes ranged from one to three stories high. In the taller Hopi houses, the family generally lived on the second floor. The first floor was used to store corn, squash, beans, sheepskins, personal articles, and the costumes, masks, and other articles necessary for Hopi ceremonies and rituals.

A Hopi home provided more than shelter. It was also an important work area. Every household contained grinding stones to process the corn grown. The resulting cornmeal was an important ingredient in nearly all Hopi dishes. In fact, occasionally platters of cornmeal were traded for other foods or items a family might need.

Either a back room of a Hopi home or a small house built close by would contain the family's *piki*

CHILDREN AND FAMILY LIFE HAVE ALWAYS BEEN IMPORTANT TO THE HOPI. HERE A YOUNG GIRL HELPS HER MOTHER WITH THE BABY. THEY'VE PLACED THE INFANT IN A CRADLEBOARD AND WRAPPED HIM IN A WOVEN BLANKET.

A HOPI WOMAN TOASTS CORNMEAL ON AN INDOOR FIRE. THIS PROCESS REMOVES EXCESS MOISTURE FROM THE FRESHLY GROUND CORN.

stone. The stone was necessary to produce piki, a thin blue cornmeal wafer eaten daily by the Hopi and used in ceremonial feasts.

To prepare piki, the stone was greased with oil and a fire was lit beneath it. The wafer batter was then spread over the hot stone. When ready, it was peeled off and turned over. The finished wafer was either folded or rolled before eaten. In addition to their piki stone, many Hopi households had a large outdoor beehive-shaped oven made of stone and adobe. The oven was used to bake bread.

Perched at the *mesa's* tip, Hopi dwellings often seemed part of the natural rock landscape. In some areas, springs flow beneath the mesa's edge. These were an important source of water for Hopi crops. Numerous villages also left large containers carved of rock outside to catch drops of rainwater. Securing water within their dry, arid environment was essential to both the Hopi's home life and their survival as a people.

FARMING AND LIVESTOCK

In early times, the Hopi depended mainly on farming for food. Every village had its own land, which was divided up and owned by the clans. Within a given clan's area, various tracts of land were allotted to the women. These parcels of land were planted and harvested by their husbands, unmarried brothers, and sons. Clans usually had land in more than one area. This protected them against *famine* if either a sudden flood or lack of rain destroyed some of their crops.

Beyond the clan lands, other fields were available for planting. Any man could develop one or more of these plots, and they remained his as long as he *cultivated* the land. Once he stopped using the fields, however, they became common ground and could be used by someone else.

Hopi farming was difficult because of the frequent droughts, high winds, and shifting sands common to the region. However, these Indian farmers learned to skillfully use the land. To shield their crops from sandstorms, they fashioned windbreakers from brush they collected. Water was scarce, so they developed the land nearest the region's largest streams, which allowed them to benefit from the overflow when a sudden cloudburst raised the water level. The Hopi also dug ditches to *irrigate* other planting areas.

In addition, the Hopi developed special varieties of plants that were capable of surviving the harsh environment. They relied on plants with deep roots because these could retain water during dry spells. Their first crops were corn (maize), beans, and cotton. After the Hopi came in contact with the Spanish, however, they learned to grow hardy kinds of peaches and apricots suited to the environment. Later, the Hopi also grew onions, chili peppers, melons, squash, pumpkins, gourds, and other fruits and vegetables.

The Hopi used whatever they planted or found growing in the wild to the fullest. Peaches, apricots, and squash were often dried and stored for when food became scarce. The Hopi also made eating utensils, containers, and ceremonial decorations out of the gourds they grew.

THE HOPI GROW A WIDE VARIETY OF CORN. THEY PLANT IT AND LATER HARVEST AND SORT IT ACCORDING TO COLOR.

The wild yucca (soapweed) plant's roots were used for cleaning, while its leaves proved well suited for making many household articles. Wild purple hair grass was used to make the brushes found in every Hopi household. While one end served as a hair-brush, the other was used to sweep the floors. These people also depended on a wide range of plants for medicines, religious ceremonies, furniture making, and dyes.

Farming and gathering materials from the wild were more essential to Hopi life than hunting. That's because large game was scarce. However, a few deer and antelope sometimes grazed nearby and were

PEACHES AND SQUASH GROWN BY THE HOPI ARE LEFT ON ROOFTOPS TO DRY IN THE SUN.

THIS PHOTOGRAPH, TAKEN AROUND 1900, SHOWS A HOPI WOMAN AND HER DAUGHTERS TENDING THE FAMILY'S SHEEP AND GOATS. LATER, THIS TASK WAS TAKEN OVER LARGELY BY HOPI MEN.

hunted by pairs of Hopi men. They also hunted the rabbits that darted about the *terrain*.

The Hopi's diet and workday changed somewhat after the sixteenth and seventeenth centuries, when the Spanish brought mules, donkeys, horses, cattle, and sheep to the region. Horse- or donkey-drawn wagons were helpful in tending fields a distance from where the family lived. Domestic animals were also good for hauling firewood and other supplies.

Some Hopi raised sheep. Their flocks and herds, however, tended to be small because of the lack of water and available grazing grounds. Unlike the farmland, there were no individually owned grazing regions.

Tending sheep involved a great deal of work, which was usually shared by several male family members. Often a father and son or two brothers worked together. In the late spring or early summer, the sheep were sheared and the wool was sold to traders.

The Hopi usually did not sell their sheep, although at times the lambs were butchered for meat. This meat was generally eaten only at special ceremonies. Whatever was left over was dried and saved for another important occasion.

Although cattle herds need less care than sheep, only a few Hopi raised cattle, which they sold or traded for profit.

HOPI CEREMONIES

Hopi ceremonies, which follow one another throughout the year, are the basis of the Hopi religion. Each Hopi village conducts its own ceremonies. The *rituals* are performed to bring rain, peace, fertility, and general well-being to the Hopi. They offer a sense of hope and tradition in a difficult natural environment.

Hopi ceremonial societies are extremely important in these undertakings. The societies are made up of individuals belonging to various clans. Hopi societies oversee the village's religious ceremonies. But each clan must still perform the ceremony that it is responsible for. The clan is also in charge of maintaining the costumes, instruments, and any materials necessary for this undertaking.

A CHILD DRESSED IN A HOPI COSTUME PREPARES TO TAKE PART IN A CEREMONY. YOUNG PEOPLE LEARN THE CUSTOMS AT AN EARLY AGE.

HERE A HOPI MAN GUARDS THE ENTRANCE OF THE ANTELOPE KIVA DURING THE SNAKE-ANTELOPE CEREMONY. HOPI CEREMONIES AND RITUALS HAVE ALWAYS BEEN EXTREMELY IMPORTANT TO THE HOPI WAY OF LIFE.

The societies support the clans in their efforts. If a clan dies out, another within the society can assume its ceremonial duties. That way the community is usually not deprived of an important ritual, although at times they still die out.

A portion of the most important ceremonies are conducted in ceremonial chambers known as *kivas*. There are several kivas in each village. These rectangular-shaped quarters are constructed either partly or completely underground. The kiva is entered through an opening on its top. Ceremony participants climb down a ladder to reach the kiva's floor.

Inside the kiva, the Hopi pray, sing, smoke, perform ancient dances, and build *altars*. Smoking is an important part of the ritual because smoke represents the desired rain clouds. Everyone who takes part in a ceremony is a member of a society, a clan, and a kiva. The major Hopi ceremonies last eight days with an extra day to begin the rituals. Important ceremonies can last even longer.

On the last days of some ceremonies, outdoor public performances may be conducted. These often include dances in the village plaza performed counterclockwise in a ceremonial ring. On some occasions, footraces are also held. A race may begin at a particular spot and end in the village. Races may be run to lead rain clouds or other gifts to the Hopi.

A HOPI MAN DRESSED AS A RITUAL CLOWN. THESE CLOWNS OFTEN PERFORM BETWEEN DANCES DURING HOPI CEREMONIES.

A number of Hopi ceremonies involve male dancers known as kachinas in colorful masks and costumes. The kachina masks are supposed to represent spirit beings. The Hopi believe that these spirits live on the mountains nearby for half the year, while spending the other half among them.

Through their prayers and offerings the Hopis send their good wishes to the spirit world. In return they hope the spirits will provide rain that will make their crops grow and ensure a fruitful year.

About seventy-five to one hundred kachinas are regularly represented in Hopi ceremonies. At times, the kachinas appear with clowns called *tsuku* or *koyew*. The clown's humorous antics and movements poke fun at human weaknesses. Their actions stress traditional Hopi ways and values.

HOPI CRAFTS

The Hopi are expert craft people. They design an assortment of objects both for daily use and special ceremonies. These include water jars, pots, bowls, and cups as well as blankets, baskets, beautifully embroidered cotton garments, moccasins, leggings, pouches, kachina dolls, and other items.

Hopi women make baskets and pottery. The men fashion leather goods and weave cotton and wool garments. These talented weavers are known for their striped woolen blankets, wedding robes, ceremonial sashes, and costumes. They often use green, black, purple, and red thread in *embroidering* traditional designs on the clothing they create.

Hopi weavers *card* their own wool and spin their own thread. They use both large and small looms depending on the size of what they weave. Hopi men also knit and crochet cotton and woolen leggings.

At the start of the twentieth century, Hopi on the various mesas began perfecting different crafts. Women from the First Mesa focused on pottery. Most did not use a potter's wheel, but instead molded the objects with their hands using clay from the area. Later, the item was polished with a stone and painted with dyes made from natural ingredients.

Early Hopi pottery often had black-on-white designs. In time, black-on-bright orange and black-on-yellow patterns became more common. While most pueblo pottery had geometric designs, the Hopis were more diverse. Their work showed human forms, animals, birds, and religious masks. Hopi pottery also depicted ceremonial events as well as symbols from their people's myths and legends. Sometimes Hopi designs reveal natural elements such as lightning, clouds, and wind. A number of modern Hopi pottery pieces include jars with black-and-red designs on orange background as well as other decorative bowls and jars.

Hopi women on the Second Mesa specialize in coiled baskets, while those on the Third Mesa are known for their wicker basketry. Some of the coiled basket work is shaped like flat plaques that may be hung on walls.

MANY HOPI WOMEN LIVING ON THE FIRST MESA SUPPLEMENT THEIR FAMILY'S INCOME BY SELLING THEIR POTTERY, SUCH AS THIS COLORFUL JAR.

To create their plaques and baskets, Second Mesa weavers pick yucca plant shoots from the wild. These are cured and dried in the sun. The shoots are then colored with natural dyes and woven into items bearing beautiful designs. The finished products are often sold or presented as gifts after important Hopi ceremonies.

Unlike those of the Second Mesa, Third Mesa weavers fashion baskets and plaques of wicker rather than yucca. They use peeled and smoothed sumac or willow stems. Their finished products are often multi-colored and depict Hopi symbols for the kachinas, sun, clouds, winds, and other natural elements.

HERE A HOPI WOMAN CREATES A WICKER BASKET PLAQUE. HER HUSBAND, SITTING NEXT TO HER, KNITS A PAIR OF LEGGINGS.

THIS SILVER NECKLACE AND CUFF BRACELET SHOW HOW TRADITIONAL HOPI DESIGNS ARE USED IN JEWELRY MAKING.

Before the mid-1940s *silversmithing* was not extremely common among the Hopi. Since then, however, they have more actively pursued this craft. Many Hopi silversmiths have brought their people's traditional designs to their work, creating a distinctive style.

Kachina dolls have also become an increasingly popular craft among the Hopi. Men carve these dolls out of cottonwood tree roots. At one time, kachinas were given only to young Hopi girls at ceremonial dances. They were used to teach Hopi young people the differences between kachinas and to better understand the importance of these spirit messengers. In recent years, however, the demand for kachinas has risen and these dolls have been extremely sought after by tourists and collectors.

A WOLF KACHINA DOLL

. . . WHEN THE WHITES CAME

Early on the Hopis did not have very much contact with the European explorers coming to the Americas. At first, the Spanish who actively claimed areas of the Southeast and Southwest met with them only in passing. In 1540, after another Pueblo tribe described the Hopi as having villages much like their own, the Spanish general Francisco Vásquez de Coronado sent a small expedition to look at the area.

Pedro de Tovar, who led the group, had heard of a large river that ran west from there. When a later expedition failed to find this quick and easy route to California, however, the Spanish did not tread on Hopi territory again for forty-three years.

In 1583, an expedition into Hopi country was led by a Spanish officer named Antonio de Espejzo.

After being cordially treated at the first Hopi village he came to, the officer claimed the land in the king of Spain's name.

Soon the Spanish became discouraged with their New Mexico and Arizona colonies. Instead of finding a land rich in natural resources, they realized that they claimed a rocky, barren terrain. Although they had hoped to somehow prosper, toward the end of the sixteenth and the beginning of the seventeenth centuries, the Spanish explorers, merchants, and military officers involved saw that they were not about to become wealthy.

In 1608, Spain even considered abandoning the area, yet there was one group of Spaniards pleased with what they found in the southwestern pueblos. These were the Roman Catholic priests who came to the Americas to establish missions. They had found a different type of wealth than that sought by the adventurer-merchants. They saw the area as rich in possible converts to Roman Catholicism.

In August 1629, Franciscan *friars* arrived in the Hopi village of Awatovi. Because the Hopi had their own strong religious beliefs, they resisted the priests' attempts to convert them. A great number of Awatovi villagers became Christians, however, after witnessing what was thought to be a miracle.

HERE FRANCISCAN FRIARS ESCORTED BY SPANISH SOLDIERS PREPARE TO ESTABLISH THEIR MISSIONS. ALTHOUGH THE INDIANS WERE PROMISED PARADISE IN HEAVEN, THEY WERE CRUELLY TREATED BY THE FRIARS ON EARTH.

According to the story, a priest had placed a cross over the eyes of a blind boy who regained his sight. No one knows whether or not the story is true, but it's certain that the Awatovi Hopi more readily accepted Christianity than the rest of their people. While several other attempts were made at establishing missions in Hopi territory, all failed. The Hopi had a strong identity as a people and continued to carry on the beliefs and practices of their ancestors.

Although the Hopi did not willingly accept the Spaniards' religion, the European intruders introduced many interesting and useful items to the region. These included unusual plant foods, silks, nails, tin, and sheet iron. Especially useful to the Hopis in fashioning both farming and craft items were the picks, crowbars, planes, and knives of iron brought by the Spanish.

Yet as the years passed, the Pueblo Indians grew increasingly resentful of Spanish domination. Often the native people were scorned and brutally dealt with by their conquerors. At times different groups rose up against the Spanish but the rebels were always quickly squelched.

In 1680, the various Pueblo Indian groups joined forces against the invaders. Acting together for the first time, they fought to drive the Spanish from New Mexico and Arizona. Following a great deal of bloodshed, the Indians finally took back the land their people had lived on for centuries.

For most of the Pueblo Indians the victory was short lived. In 1692 the Spanish returned, determined to recover the area they lost. Although they recaptured the New Mexico pueblos, the Hopi

IN 1680, PUEBLO INDIANS BRAVELY FOUGHT AGAINST THE INVADING SPANISH SOLDIERS. DESPITE THE SOLDIERS' SUPERIOR ARMOR AND ARMS, THE INDIANS DEFEATED THEM FOR A TIME.

remained free. Their success was a result of a number of factors. Being farther away and more geographically remote than the other pueblos, they were extremely difficult to reach. Following the 1680 revolt, the Hopi had also moved their villages from the mesa's foot to its narrowly edged top. While they had to carry water up to their new location daily, they were in an excellent position to resist attacks.

The Hopi were further assisted in fending off the returning Spaniards by Indians from other pueblos who now lived among them. These Indians joined the Hopi after refusing to remain under Spanish domination.

Because Spanish merchants and traders had never been very interested in the out-of-the-way Hopi villages, it was largely priests backed by Spanish soldiers that the Hopi hoped to avoid. Following the pueblo revolt, Awatovi, the village where a blind boy supposedly regained his sight through a priest, was the only Hopi village that embraced Christianity. However, the other Hopi refused to accept this. As a result, in the winter of 1700–1701 they attacked Awatovi. According to accounts of the raid, village men were killed while the women and children were taken captive. The village's church was also destroyed.

The Santa Fe governor sent troops to punish the Hopi for ransacking the Christian village. The Indians proved to be militarily superior, however, and were victorious. The Hopi also defeated two other military expeditions. Then, nine years later, at the urging of some Franciscan friars, the governor launched his broadest attack against the Hopi. A number of Indians were killed in the bloody battle, but the Hopis pushed the soldiers back and remained free.

Meanwhile, the king of Spain had become increasingly discouraged over the Franciscans' failure in converting the Hopi. So in 1741 he asked Jesuit priests (another religious order) to try to bring Christianity to these people. The Jesuits weren't overly enthusiastic about their new assignment and never even reached the distant Hopi villages.

Anxious to renew their efforts, the Franciscans submitted false reports to the king indicating that they had finally won over a large number of Hopi converts. Despite continued pressure, the Hopi refused to give up their beliefs. Unlike many tribes, they succeeded in keeping their culture intact through the years.

Even by the middle of the nineteenth century, Hopi villages remained somewhat isolated due to their distance from Pueblo groups such as those in the Rio Grande area. Yet the Hopi were hardly carefree. Although they defeated the Spanish conquerors, they rarely enjoyed long periods of peace.

A FRANCISCAN MISSION SIMILAR TO MANY ESTABLISHED THROUGHOUT THE SOUTHWEST. THE FRIARS HOPED TO CONVERT THE INDIANS, BUT MOST HOPIS FIERCELY HELD TO THEIR TRADITIONAL BELIEFS.

THE DRY BARREN LAND AND POOR GROWING CONDITIONS MADE FARMING DIFFICULT FOR THE HOPI, BUT IT ALSO MADE THEIR TERRITORY LESS DESIRABLE TO THE ENCROACHING EUROPEANS.

Unfortunately, the tribe was subjected to ongoing attacks from both Mexicans and hostile neighboring Indian tribes such as the Apache and Navajo. These raiders robbed and plundered Hopi villages. They frequently took captives to sell into slavery in Mexico.

The situation in the southwest dramatically changed after 1848, however. The United States defeated Mexico in the Mexican War and acquired what is now most of Arizona and parts of New Mexico in addition to a sizable amount of other territory. That meant that for the first time the Hopi would have to deal with the U.S. government.

In some ways, the Hopi were more fortunate than other American Indians. Because of their land's lack of mineral wealth and poor growing conditions white settlers did not quickly seize their territory. Nevertheless, with the U.S. government's takeover, whites increasingly entered the region. Yet unfortunately the Navajo attacks continued. So, in 1850, a group of seven Hopi leaders journeyed to Santa Fe for their first conference with the official Indian agent John S. Calhoun. They were anxious to see if the new white government could curb the frequent Navajo raids.

Their answer came the following year in 1851, when the military outpost Fort Defiance was established. Although it was built largely to protect white settlers from Navajo raiders, the Hopi benefited as well. Once the Civil War began, however, most of the fort's soldiers were needed elsewhere and withdrawn. The Navajo attacks reached new heights during this period with an especially fierce onslaught on the fort itself in 1860. The Hopi suffered as a result of the increased Navajo plundering. And to worsen the situation, a small band of white settlers attacked several villages mistakenly thinking that the Hopi were responsible for the raids.

The Hopi's well-being was further threatened in 1864 by a severe drought. The Indians were extremely concerned because a prolonged dry spell usually brought widespread famine. Hoping to keep from starving, a group of Hopi approached the U.S. governor to ask for help.

Sadly, the whites misunderstood the Hopi's intentions and threw them in jail before they could explain their purpose. Although the Indians were released shortly thereafter, they were justly angry and insulted by the way they had been treated. The Hopi received no government assistance, and when famine struck in 1866, large numbers of their people died. The death count climbed even higher after several infected white soldiers visiting the villages accidentally started a smallpox epidemic.

THE HOPI TRIED TO PRESERVE THEIR ANCESTORS' WAYS AND WANTED THEIR CHILDREN TO DO THE SAME. HERE A MOTHER FASHIONED HER DAUGHTER'S HAIR AS UNMARRIED HOPI GIRLS TRADITIONALLY WORE IT. THE GIRL'S HAIR HAS BEEN WOUND OVER WOODEN HAIR BOWS.

Meanwhile, more whites continued to venture into Hopi country. By 1885, the Atlantic and Pacific Railroad made its way through northern Arizona and Mormon and Baptist missions were established there as well. However, there were still few religious converts among the Hopi. And as the Mormons increasingly took over their land, the native people's resentment grew.

With the railroad bringing large numbers of whites to the region, new white towns and settlements soon sprang up. Unfortunately, most of the newcomers looked down on the Indians who'd been there for hundreds of years and felt there was little to learn from them. The growing population made it necessary for the U.S. government to establish formal boundaries between white and Indian land. On December 16, 1882, President Chester A. Arthur signed an order formally establishing a Hopi *reservation.*

In addition to outside pressures, the Hopi also had to deal with tensions from within. While some Hopi were more accepting of increased contact with whites, others felt it crucial that they hold on to their traditions. This division continued, and in 1887 a group of Hopi parents and their leaders were imprisoned for not permitting their children to attend a government-run reservation school. Even as late as

PRESIDENT CHESTER A. ARTHUR SIGNED AN EXECUTIVE ORDER CREATING THE HOPI RESERVATION. THE AREA SET ASIDE MEASURED ABOUT 55 BY 70 MILES (88 BY 112 KM).

1911, military force was used to ensure that Hopi young people went to the reservation school.

Although many Hopi tried to spurn white influences, it was often difficult to do so. Nevertheless, in keeping with their people's respect for peace, only a tenth of the Hopi served in the U.S. Army during World War I. And with the outbreak of World War II, large numbers of Hopi registered as conscientious objectors. Rather than fight, they offered to do nonviolent service. As they explained their feelings, ". . . our way requires us to conduct our lives in friendship and peace, without anger, without greed, without wickedness of any kind among ourselves or in our association with any people. . . ."

After the war, the Hopi's lifestyle was clearly not what it had been fifty years before. Many Hopi left the reservation to find work in neighboring towns and cities. Instead of farming, a large number of Hopi now earned a wage with which to support themselves and their families.

The Hopi tried to remain strong as a people, but at times they faced difficult obstacles. On numerous

HOPI INDIANS PERFORM A DANCE TO GIVE THANKS. THEY RESISTED PRESSURE FROM EUROPEANS AND OTHERS TO ABANDON SUCH PRACTICES.

A GROUP OF HOPI MEET TO DISCUSS IMPORTANT ISSUES CONCERNING PEOPLE.

occasions they felt that their special relationship to the land was seriously threatened by outsiders.

They were also divided on how to handle these situations. One segment revived the Hopi Tribal Council, a group that hoped to effectively use the U.S. legal system to achieve their goals. Other Hopi disagreed with this approach. Many of the traditional elders still thought of their people as an independent Indian nation. They stressed that the Hopi had never even signed a peace treaty with the U.S. government. Regardless of how the different factions chose to handle the problem, both sides were committed to doing the best for their people.

To protect their land and way of life, the Hopi have fought against the Navajos encroaching on their territory. Traditional Hopi also actively opposed environmentally dangerous strip-mining projects, explaining that the area is "part of the heart of our Mother Earth." They insisted that "if the land is abused, the sacred Hopi way of life will disappear."

Undeniably, contact with white society has had an effect on the Hopi. Observing tribal traditions varies from village to village as well as among individuals. Many Hopi now depend less on growing or making life's basic necessities. Often modern young couples choose to live in their own homes rather than with relatives.

Yet through the centuries the Hopi have successfully combined new ways with ongoing traditions. While cinder blocks now often replace the ancient stones of their homes, within these dwellings valued Hopi customs continue.

Although many Hopi craftspeople and artists work at other jobs to support themselves and their families, their art still reflects traditional Hopi themes. Corn and other crops continue to be grown on the reservation, and each morning, at dawn, Hopi men and women can be seen sprinkling cornmeal on the ground as an offering to the gods believed to rise with the sun.

In addition to cultivating crops, the Hopi also rely on wild plants. Through the years they've learned which plants have medicinal value. These natural drugs are used to soothe an upset stomach, ease an earache, or heal a rash, as well as for other purposes. Hopi healers at the reservation are still sought out and do not charge a fee for their services. Although most Hopi use formally trained doctors and technicians, at times ancient and modern health care practices are combined. A number of Hopi healers have earned the respect of doctors who call upon them as an added resource for their patients.

But perhaps Hopi children best represent their people's future. Children are highly valued among the Hopi, and those under eighteen make up about 60 percent of the population. There is a strong emphasis on education, resulting in an almost zero school dropout rate for Hopi youths.

In many ways, these young people reflect a successful blend of the past and present. They eat traditional Hopi foods but also enjoy Popsicles and chocolate bars. They listen to rock music, but still sing their people's songs. They participate in after-school activities but nevertheless like wearing traditional Hopi garments in village dances.

A HOPI BOY PERFORMS THE HOOP DANCE AT A FESTIVAL. HOPI YOUTHS REPRESENT THE SPIRIT OF THEIR PEOPLE'S FUTURE.

Many Hopi still strive to preserve their ancient rituals and values. Their respect for the past and the things that make their people special is evident in their crafts, ceremonies, and beliefs. The Hopi remain a proud people, with a strong sense of identity and purpose.

GLOSSARY

Altar a raised structure used in religious rites

Card to comb out wool fibers before spinning them

Clan a group of related people

Cultivate to prepare and use land through plowing and sowing

Embroidering decorative needlework

Famine a serious shortage or lack of food

Friar a member of a religious order

Irrigate to supply land with water through ditches or other means

Kachina doll a small figure, generally made of wood, that represents the kachinas, or spirit beings, of the Hopi and other Indians of the American Southwest

Kiva a ceremonial chamber

Koyew a Hopi clown that performs at some ceremonies; also known as **Tsuku**

Mesa a high, broad plateau with sharp, rocky slopes

Piki stone a stone used for cooking on which corn wafers are made

Plunder the act of robbing

Pueblo the Spanish word for town

Reservation land set aside for Indian use

Ritual a religious act

Silversmithing working with silver

Terrain a land area

Tiponi a stone or wooden object symbolizing a clan's spirit protector

FOR FURTHER READING

Anderson, Peter. *Maria Martinez: Pueblo Potter*. Chicago: Childrens Press, 1992.

Avery, Susan, and Linda Skinner. *Extraordinary American Indians*. Chicago: Childrens Press, 1992.

Ayer, Eleanor H. *The Anasazi*. New York: Walker, 1993.

Bahti, Mark. *Southwestern Indian Arts and Crafts*. Las Vegas, Nev.: KC Publications, 1989.

Carey, Valerie Scho. *Quail Song: A Pueblo Indian Tale*. New York: Putnam, 1990.

Keegan, Marcia. *Pueblo Boy: Growing Up in Two Worlds*. New York: Cobblehill, 1991.

Lavitt, Edward, and Robert E. McDowell. *Nihancan's Feast of Beaver: Animal Tales of the North American Indians*. Sante Fe, N.M.: Museum of New Mexico, 1990.

Liptak, Karen. *Indians of the Southwest*. New York: Facts On File, 1991.

Swentzell, Rina. *Children of Clay: A Family of Pueblo Potters*. Chicago: Lerner, 1992.

White Deer of Autumn. *The Native American Book of Knowledge*. Hillsboro, Ore.: Beyond Words, 1992.

———. *The Native American Book of Life*. Hillsboro, Ore.: Beyond Words, 1992.

INDEX

Italicized page numbers refer to illustrations.

ABOUT THE AUTHOR

Elaine Landau has been a newspaper reporter, a children's book editor, and a youth services librarian. She has written over sixty books for young people, including *The Sioux*, *The Cherokees*, *The Pomo*, and *The Chilula*. Ms. Landau makes her home in Sparta, New Jersey.